B❍❍ks Al❍ud!

Experiencing books and reading aloud with

and The Free Library of Philadelphia

Sponsored by The William Penn Foundation

D1303237

teddy bears

abc

susanna gretz

FOUR WINDS PRESS   NEW YORK

a

arriving

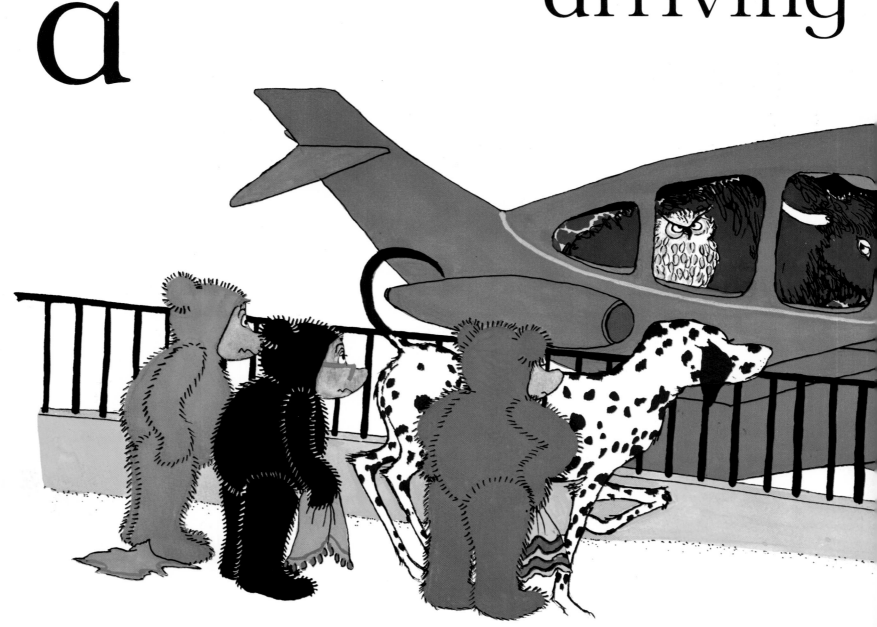

in an airplane

b building

C climbing

d

dancing

e

eating

f finding fleas in their fur

g

gargling

h

hiding

i

idling

j jumping

k keeping kangaroos in the kitchen

1 leaping into the leaves

m

mucking in mud

n

napping

O opening oatmeal

p

painting

q

quarreling

r

running

in the rain

S

swimming

t   tickling in a tent

u
unwrapping an umbrella

V vanishing

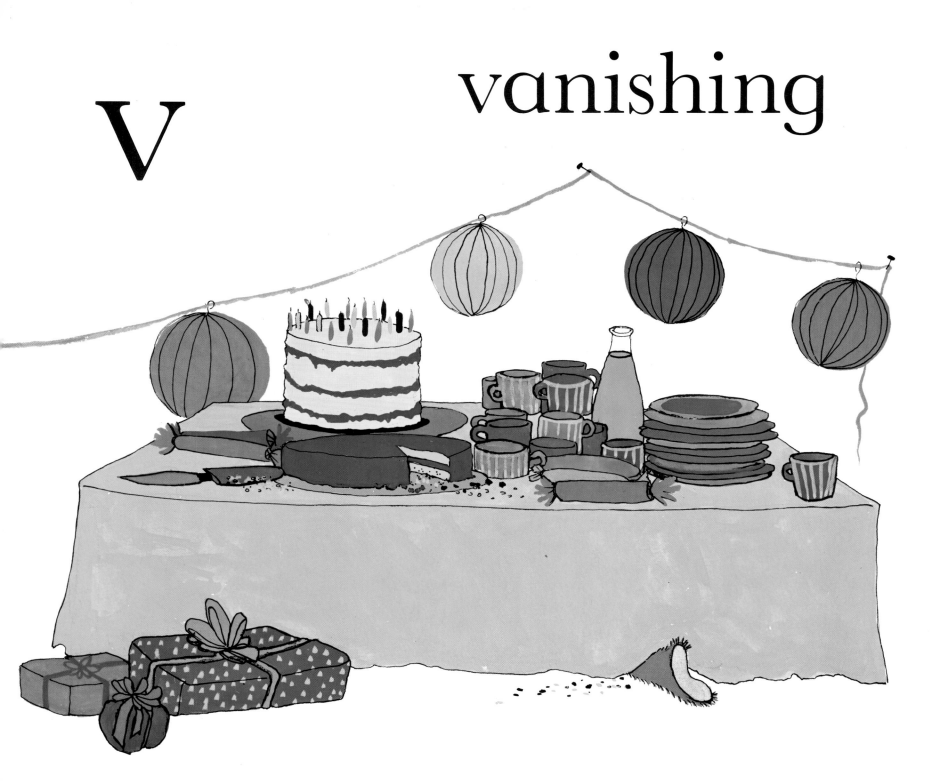

W

washing

X being x-rayed

y yelling at a yak

z

zipping off

to the zoo

Four Winds Press, Macmillan Publishing Company, 866 Third Avenue, New York, NY 10022. Collier Macmillan Canada, Inc. Printed in Great Britain. First published in 1974 by Ernest Benn Ltd, London. First Four Winds Press edition 1986.

10 9 8 7 6 5 4 3

Library of Congress Cataloging-in-Publication Data   Gretz, Susanna. Teddy bears abc. Summary: The letters of the alphabet describe the various activities of five teddy bears, from arriving in an airplane to zipping off to the zoo. [1. Teddy bears—Fiction. 2. Alphabet] I. Title.
PZ7.G8636Tg 1986   [E]   86-4742   ISBN 0-02-738130-7

Printed in Singapore by Imago Publishing Ltd